The Jungle Book

Retold by

Saviour Pirotta

Illustrated by

Alex Paterson

ARCTURUS

For Jode Paton—SP.

For Alexa and William—AP.

ARCTURUS

This edition published in 2018 by Arcturus Publishing Limited
26/27 Bickels Yard, 151–153 Bermondsey Street,
London SE1 3HA

Writer: Saviour Pirotta
Illustrator: Alex Paterson
Designer: Jeni Child
Editor: Sebastian Rydberg
Art Director: Jessica Crass

ISBN: 978-1-78828-691-6
CH006179NT
Supplier 24, Date 0318, Print run 6739

Printed in Malaysia

Contents

CHAPTER 1

Man Cub Joins the Pack

It was late evening when Father Wolf woke up from his nap. He looked around the cave. His four cubs were playing happily. Mother Wolf was licking behind their ears as they tumbled in the dust.

Suddenly, there was a loud roar outside the cave. The wolf cubs stopped playing at once. Their eyes widened with fear.

"It's Shere Khan, the tiger," whispered Mother Wolf. "He sounds very angry."

"He must be hungry," said Father Wolf.

"Don't worry," Mother Wolf comforted the cubs. "We're safe in here. The entrance to our cave is too narrow for him."

A shadow appeared in the mouth of the cave. It was Tabaqui, the jackal.

"Father Wolf," he said. "Do you have anything to eat in there?"

"There are some bones at the back of the cave," replied Father Wolf. "But there's no meat on them."

"They'll do for an old starving jackal like me," said Tabaqui. He crunched noisily on the bones. "Did you hear the news about the terrible Shere Khan? He's moved to this part of the jungle. It's closer to the village, and that gives him a better chance of catching a man cub."

"He shouldn't be in this part of the jungle at all," growled Father Wolf. "Not without warning us first. The people from the village are sure to come looking for him. I don't want man hunters finding my family's cave."

"He's been chasing a man cub all day," said Tabaqui. "But he's lame, as you know, and the man cub got away. Shere Khan accidentally stepped in a fire chasing him. He's burned his paw. That's made him even more angry than usual."

There was another tiger roar outside, and something on two legs came tottering into the cave. It was a man cub and it looked frightened.

Shere Khan's angry face blocked the light at the mouth of the cave. "Is the man cub in there?" he roared.

"What if he is?" answered Mother Wolf bravely.

"I've been chasing that man cub and his parents all day," growled Shere Khan. "The parents got back to their village. But the boy ran the other way. He is in there, I know it. GIVE HIM TO ME."

Mother Wolf gently drew the man cub deeper into the cave. "We shall do no such thing, you brute. Pick on someone your own size."

"You'll never get the man cub, I promise you that," snapped Father Wolf.

Shere Khan tried to get into the cave, squirming his powerful shoulders. His enormous paws raked the air. But he knew it was no use. The entrance to the cave really was too narrow.

"This is not the end of the matter," he spat. "I WILL get my paws on the man cub."

"The man cub will learn the ways of the wolf," said Father Wolf. "And when he is a man, he will come and hunt you down. The jungle will be rid of Shere Khan forever."

"Now, go back to your own part of the jungle," added Mother Wolf. "And leave my family in peace."

Shere Khan limped away, howling with rage. When the coast was clear, Tabaqui left the cave, too. Mother Wolf licked the

man cub's hair. He looked funny with
fur only on his head. "He must get very
cold at night," she said.

The man cub cuddled up to Mother
Wolf for warmth. The four cubs licked
his hair to be friendly. Soon, the man cub
had forgotten all about Shere Khan. He
tumbled around the cave with the cubs.

"What shall we call him?" wondered
Father Wolf.

"He reminds me of a hairless frog," said
Mother Wolf. "We'll call him Mowgli."

On the night of the full moon, Mother and Father Wolf took the four cubs to Council Rock. They took Mowgli with them, too, because now he was part of the family.

Council Rock was a hilltop in the jungle. Here, the wolves met to inspect the new cubs before they were allowed to join the pack.

Akela, the leader of the pack, was lying on top of Council Rock. He was a powerful wolf with amber eyes. Below him, some forty wolves sat in a circle. They were inspecting the cubs.

Father Wolf pushed his four cubs into the circle. The older wolves watched them closely as they played and chased each other. At last, one of them nodded. "They shall be proud members of our pack."

Mother Wolf nudged Mowgli forward.

He sat in the circle, playing with pebbles.

"The man cub has no right to be in a wolf pack," roared a voice behind the rock. "I chased him across the jungle. Hand him over to me."

It was Shere Khan. He'd been watching the meeting from behind a tree.

"But Mowgli has lived with us for over two weeks," said Mother Wolf. "He is part of our family."

"He might be part of your family," argued some of the other wolves. "But we don't want him in the pack. He doesn't even have any fur."

"Silence," called Akela. "You know the rules. If there are two here who are not part of his family but can speak for Mowgli, he can join the pack."

Mother Wolf looked around the hilltop. Who would speak for man son? A sleepy bear stepped forward. His name was Baloo. He taught the wolf cubs the laws of the jungle and was the only animal allowed to attend wolf meetings.

"Let him stay," he said. "I shall be his teacher."

"But we need another to speak for Mowgli," said Akela. "Who will it be?"

There was a rustle in the trees, and

Bagheera, the black panther, slunk out. "I have no right to be in this meeting," he purred. "But I couldn't help overhearing. To prevent a cub from joining your pack because he has no fur is a mistake. It is not his fault he is hairless. Accept him, and I shall be a teacher to him, too."

Mother and Father Wolf looked at each other and smiled. At last, Mowgli was part of the pack.

CHAPTER 2
Beware of the Monkeys

Time passed, and Mowgli grew into a
strong, healthy boy. Father Wolf taught
him how to recognize the sounds of the
forest. Baloo showed him how to pick
nuts and how to climb up trees for fruit.

When Mowgli wanted
a treat, Baloo helped
pick honey without
disturbing the bees.
Often, Mowgli
would go fishing in the river. On sunny
days, he swam in the cool water and slept
on the rocks in the sunshine. Bagheera
would tell him stories of the village where
the people lived. Bagheera often went
there at night, looking for hens to steal.

He didn't always come back with prey, but he learned a lot about how people behaved and what they did.

"I have to be very careful when I'm hunting," he said. "Man has a precious red flower that is hot to the touch. He calls it fire. It scares me."

The wolf pack grew to like Mowgli. When they had thorns in their paws, Mowgli would remove them with his nails.

Only one beast watched him with hate in his eyes. That was Shere Khan, the tiger.

One day, Mowgli would not sit still for his lessons. Baloo was trying to teach him how to hiss like a snake. Baloo got angry. He smacked Mowgli on the bottom.

"Ouch," said Bagheera, who had dropped by to watch the lesson. "The poor boy's black and blue. Leave him alone, Baloo. You're going to kill him."

"I just gave him a gentle bear pat," argued Baloo. "Mowgli has to learn how important bird calls are. Animal calls, too. One day, he might find himself in danger and need to make one of those calls."

"But I know them all already," groaned Mowgli, rubbing his bottom.

"Well, show me how a snake hisses, then," said Bagheera.

Mowgli stuck out his tongue and hissed very loudly. "Hissssssss! Hissssss!"

"My, that's very good," said the black panther. "I almost looked behind me, expecting to see a real snake."

"Now show Uncle Bagheera how you would call a kite."

A kite was a very large bird. It had a call that could be heard from far away. Mowgli cleared his throat and called out. "Twee-eek! Twee-eek."

"Ha," said Bagheera. "That sounds just like my old friend Rann. He's a wise kite. You're learning fast, Mowgli. Well done!"

"The monkeys think I'm clever, too," boasted Mowgli.

Baloo, who'd been resting against a tree, sat up. "You have been talking to the monkeys? They are not to be trusted."

"But they give me nuts and bananas!"

"They don't give you fruit because they're kind," warned Baloo. "They're always up to mischief. The monkeys don't obey the law of the jungle. That is why the other animals don't speak to them. Promise me you'll never to talk to them again."

Mowgli promised. The sun got hotter and Baloo, Bagheera, and Mowgli found a shady spot to sleep in. Soon, Baloo and Bagheera were snoring.

Mowgli heard chattering in the trees above him.

"Hee-hee-hee. These nuts are crunchy."

"Hee-hee-hee. Absolutely delicious."

It was the monkeys. Mowgli desperately wanted some nuts, but he had promised Baloo he would not talk to them. He closed his eyes and tried very hard to go to sleep.

"Hee-hee-hee," came a voice from the tree branches. "Man cub is fast asleep."

"Hee-hee-hee," tittered a second voice. "Let's get him. We need someone to show us how to weave wind breakers out of reeds. Man cub will do that. He weaves wind breakers for the wolves."

Suddenly, Mowgli felt furry paws all over his arms and legs. They hauled him up into the branches of the trees. "Help," he shouted. "I'm being kidnapped. Help!"

His shouting woke up Baloo and Bagheera. Bagheera growled fiercely and leaped up the tree. But the monkeys beat him down again. There were so many of them, Bagheera could not fight back.

Baloo watched helplessly as Mowgli's

feet disappeared into the tree canopy.
He howled and beat his head against the
tree trunk, making it shake.

"Mowgli! Kidnapped by vile monkeys!"

Up in the treetops, Mowgli was terribly
frightened. The monkeys were hauling
him from one tree to another. The treetops
grew so close together, Mowgli couldn't
see the forest below. But he knew it would
be a long way down if he fell. He hoped
the monkeys wouldn't let go of him.

"Hee-hee-hee," chattered one of the
monkeys. "Aren't we clever? We managed
to snatch man cub right from under
Baloo and Bagheera's nose."

Mowgli tried to think. Where were
these horrible monkeys taking him? What
did they want from him? And how could
he escape?

At last, the monkeys stopped to rest. They lay back on the tree branches and closed their eyes for a nap. Their tails swung back and forth as they snoozed.

Mowgli looked up at the sky. The sun was setting, and the clouds seemed to be on fire. And there, soaring high up in the air, was Rann, the kite—Bagheera's friend!

Suddenly, Mowgli knew what he had to do. He put his hands around his mouth and called out. "Twee-eek! Twee-eek!" It was the bird call Baloo had taught him.

Rann heard the call and answered. "Twee-eek! Twee-eek!" He spotted Mowgli far below and swooped down toward him.

"Why do you call, man cub?" he asked, settling down on a tree branch close to Mowgli.

"I've been kidnapped by the monkeys,"

whispered Mowgli. "Please find Baloo
and Bagheera. Will you tell them where
the monkeys are taking me? They might
come to rescue me."

Rann flapped his wings to rise back
up in the air. He watched from the skies
as the monkeys pulled Mowgli back into
the treetops. He followed at a distance as
the monkeys made their way through the
trees. And then, he set off to find Baloo
and Bagheera.

CHAPTER 3

The Scary City

Baloo sat howling. "My poor man cub!"

"We need to think, not howl," said Bagheera, "or we might never see poor Mowgli again."

Just then, he spotted Rann swooping down out of the sky. "I have a message from Mowgli," said the kite. "He has been kidnapped by the monkeys."

"We know that," wailed Baloo. "But we don't know where they have taken him."

"I followed them," said Rann. "They're holding him prisoner in Cold Lairs."

Cold Lairs had once been a beautiful city. Kings and queens had lived there. They had received people from all over the world in it. But then, the royals moved away.

Now Cold Lairs was just a long-abandoned ruin—and haunted! No animal ever set foot in it except the monkeys, who were too stupid to be scared of ghosts.

"How can we get there?" asked Baloo.

"My friend Khaa, the python, will take us," said Bagheera. "He knows every inch of the jungle. And the monkeys are terrified of him. One look at his powerful coils, and they'll let Mowgli go."

In Cold Lairs, the monkeys set Mowgli down in a great courtyard. They danced in a circle around him. "Teach us how to make wind breakers out of reeds," they said, "or we'll feed you to the ghosts."

"I'll gladly teach you," said Mowgli. "But first, you must give me something to eat. I'm hungry."

The monkeys went away to fetch some nuts. There was a lot of chattering as they argued over who should pick them. In the end, no one did. The monkeys started fighting.

Mowgli set off to find some himself. He walked across the courtyard past a throne where the king used to sit. He peeped into a stable where once the queen's elephants were kept. At last, he came to a garden full of fruit trees.

"Look out!" shouted one of the monkeys. "The man cub is escaping."

The monkeys swarmed all over Mowgli and dragged him into the king's old summerhouse. There was a clang as the monkeys slammed the gate shut. One of them turned the key in a padlock.

Mowgli looked around him. The summerhouse was full of snakes, and they were all hissing and glaring at him.

Mowgli froze for a moment. The snakes were crawling toward him. Their tongues flickered. Then, Mowgli remembered the snake call Baloo had taught him.

"Hisssssssss!"

The snakes stopped wagging their tongues.

"Hissssssssss!" went Mowgli again.

The snakes stopped crawling toward him. One of them raised his head and answered Mowgli's call. "Hisssss!"

Mowgli sighed with relief. The snakes knew he was a friend. They would not hurt him now.

It got dark. The monkeys fell asleep in the ruins. Some snored loudly. From the corner of his eye, Mowgli saw a shadow creep across the palace wall.

He recognized it at once. It was Bagheera. Rann had fetched him.

There was a loud roar as Bagheera started hitting out at the monkeys. The creatures woke up and fought back fiercely, crawling all over the panther. They pinched, poked, and bit his back.

But Bagheera had fought bigger enemies than monkeys. He roared again and lashed out with his terrible claws. The monkeys on his back went flying up in the air, howling and screeching.

The other monkeys fell back, muttering.

"I'm here to save you, man cub," shouted Bagheera. He'd spotted Mowgli in the summerhouse. "And I am not alone."

A moment later, the palace wall shook and came tumbling down. Baloo had arrived. He had knocked a hole in the wall to get into the garden.

Baloo grunted and started ripping monkeys off Bagheera's back. Their screeches drew more monkeys to the fight. They hurled themselves at Baloo from every corner. Mowgli could hardly see the poor bear under the sea of

monkey fur. He wished he could break out of the summerhouse to help him.

For a while, it looked like Baloo would be finished. There were too many monkeys. But then, a terrible sound echoed across the garden. "Sssssssssssssss!"

The monkeys stopped chattering at once and looked around them in alarm.

Through the trees came the dreaded shape of Khaa, the python. The moon shone on his scaly skin, and his eyes glimmered like two jewels. The monkeys backed away, their teeth chattering in panic.

Khaa swung his head from side to side. He fixed the monkeys with his deadly stare. "Sssstay you sssooo," he hissed.

The monkeys all froze like statues. They tried to move, but they couldn't. The python had hypnotized them.

He wrapped
his coil around
one monkey
to make sure
his powers had

worked. The monkey didn't even flinch.
It stood as stiff as a straw doll.

Khaa hissed at Baloo and Bagheera.
"Get the man cub out of here while my
spell lasts."

Baloo growled at Mowgli. "Stand
aside, man cub." He threw himself at the
enormous gate, and it came crashing
down in the grass. "Come on," he said
to Mowgli. "Let's get you home."

Mowgli turned to Khaa. "Thank you
for your help! I would still be a prisoner
if it were not for you."

"I admire your free spirit, man cub,"

said the python. "Perhaps you will come to my help one day."

"If you ever need me, come look for me," replied Mowgli. "I would be very happy to help you."

Khaa flicked his tongue and slid up to the monkeys. "You sssssshall dancceeeeee," he hissed. "And you will keep on dancing till the sun comes up."

As Bagheera carried Mowgli out of the garden on his back, the monkeys started moving. At first they, swayed slowly. Then, they began stomping and chattering.

And they went on dancing till the sun rose, and Mowgli and his friends had escaped.

CHAPTER 4

Fire! Fire!

Mowgli and Bagheera started spending a lot of time together. They explored the deepest parts of the jungle, where no one else had gone before.

Late one night, they sat together on a moonlit rock. "Remember I once told you about Man's red flower?" asked Bagheera.

Mowgli nodded. "Fire."

"You might need it soon—Akela is getting old," he explained. "Soon, he will not be able to lead the wolf pack anymore. There are younger wolves desperate to take his place. Some of them are friends with Shere Khan. They don't like you."

"I've never done any of them any harm," said Mowgli sadly. "The wolves all come to me when they have thorns in their paws."

"Man has a power that scares the jungle animals," said Bagheera. "Look into my eyes."

Mowgli stared into Bagheera's eyes. After a while, the panther hung his head. "All men and women have that power in their eyes. The wolves are scared of it. They hate you for it. One day, they will try to destroy you."

Bagheera lifted up his head, so that Mowgli could see his neck. "Look closely. What do you see?"

"A scar," replied Mowgli. "The fur around it has been rubbed away."

"I was once captured by menfolk," said Bagheera. "They kept me in chains because they were scared of me. I don't tell anyone in the jungle about it. It's my shameful secret. I got used to living in the man village, but deep in my heart I knew I would one day escape and come back. And I did. Do you know why? Because the jungle is my home. It's where I belong. And you belong in the man village, with the people who walk on two legs. One day, you must go back to them."

"But the jungle is my home," argued Mowgli.

Bagheera sighed. "The wolves are having a secret meeting soon. Go fetch the red flower before it's too late."

When it got dark, Mowgli crept to the man village. He watched carefully from the bushes as a family sat around the fire. They were sharing a meal. When they finished, the mother led them all indoors. Only one girl remained to look after the fire.

Mowgli crept up behind her. The moment her head was turned, he snatched the fire pot and raced back to the jungle.

The secret meeting at Council Rock took place on the next full moon. Akela was there. He looked old and tired.

Shere Khan slunk out of the trees.

"What are you doing here?" asked Akela.

"I come for the man cub," growled Shere Khan. "Surely, you must have grown tired of him. He is not really one of you."

"We accepted him as a member of the pack," replied Akela firmly.

Shere Khan's roar shook the trees. "Give me to him, or I shall hunt down every single animal in your part of the jungle. There will be nothing left for any of you to eat. You will all starve."

"Let him have the man cub, Akela," said the younger wolves. "The tiger is right. Mowgli is not a wolf like us."

Akela sighed wearily. "I shall make a deal with you, Tiger. You can become the leader of the pack instead of me—if you promise never to hurt the man cub."

The younger wolves gathered around Shere Khan, wagging their tails.

"Shere Khan for leader!" they cried. "With the mighty Shere Khan leading us, we shall hunt and kill as we please. We shall be the most feared animals in the entire jungle."

"No," shouted Mowgli, leaping out from behind a tree. "You are wolves. Your leader should be a wolf. Don't let the tiger fool you. He will eat you all one by one."

"Seize the boy!" roared Shere Khan.

"Don't be scared," Bagheera hissed at Mowgli. "Remember your secret weapon."

The growling wolves surrounded Mowgli. Their jaws snapped, and their eyes glowed like embers. But Mowgli knew what he had to do. He'd brought the pot of glowing charcoal with him. Now, he thrust a branch into it, setting it on fire. He swung the burning branch in a big circle around him.

The wolves backed away at once; their growling turned to whimpering.

"Red Flower," they whispered.

"Come on, Shere Khan," shouted Mowgli.

"I'm here for you to eat."

He lunged at the tiger and thrust the burning branch under his nose. Shere Khan's whiskers burst into flames. He leapt back, batting away at his whiskers with his paws. "I will kill you for this." And then, he turned tail and disappeared into the jungle. Most of the other wolves followed him. Only a few remained. They were the ones who had welcomed Mowgli into the pack.

Bagheera came out from the trees. Mowgli's wolf parents and his four brothers gathered around him.

"I shall go and live in the man village," said Mowgli. "It is not safe for me here anymore. But I'll be back one day, you'll see. And I promise you this: I will bring Shere Khan's tiger skin with me."

"Goodbye, my child," cried Mother Wolf, giving Mowgli a lick on the face. "Take care of yourself, and remember, you have grown up with wolves. You are as cunning as we are. I shall think of you every day."

"Goodbye, my son," said Father Wolf. "Always be brave like I have taught you."

"I shall come see you when I can slip out of the jungle unnoticed," said the eldest of the wolf cubs, who was called

Brother Wolf. "I shall bring you news of the jungle."

Mowgli felt strange drops of water running down his face.

"Bagheera," he gasped, "My eyes are leaking. I am dying."

"Those are only tears," said the black panther gently. "You are crying. All human beings do. Goodbye, man cub. Remember all the animal calls that Baloo and I taught you. You must never forget them."

Then, he turned and started walking slowly away.

CHAPTER 5

Mowgli in the Man Village

An old man was standing at the village gate when Mowgli arrived. Mowgli had not eaten for a long time. He was very hungry and thirsty. But he didn't know the man words for food and drink. He pointed to his mouth and opened it wide.

The old man did not understand. "Help! Wild animal! Wild animal!" he called. "This creature is going to eat me up."

Children and grown-ups came running. They crowded around Mowgli, staring at his shaggy hair and long nails. Someone poked him with a stick.

"The creature is dirty."

"Its fur is all matted."

The headman of the village came out

to see why the villagers were making so much noise. "Why, it's a human child."

A woman pushed through the crowds. She held out her arms to Mowgli. "I lost a boy in the jungle many years ago. A tiger took him. He would be this boy's age if he had survived. Perhaps this is my son."

She took Mowgli's hand. "Come, I will look after you. You shall be as a son to me."

Mowgli didn't understand a word Messua said, but she looked friendly. Her eyes were full of kindness, so he followed her.

 Messua could tell Mowgli was very hungry. She gave him some milk to drink. Mowgli sniffed at it suspiciously. He had never tasted milk before.

"Drink," Messua encouraged him.

Mowgli drank. Messua gave him some flatbread to eat. Then, she took him down to the stream to wash. She cut his hair and combed it neatly.

While she combed, she taught Mowgli a few words. "Hello" and "Please" and "Thank you."

At bedtime, she laid out a clean sheet on a cot.

"Sleep. Rest."

Mowgli lay down, but he couldn't sleep.

 He had never slept under a roof before. He felt closed in. It worried him that he could not see the stars twinkling in the sky.

When Messua was asleep, he carried the cot outside. The man village was very quiet. Mowgli missed the sounds of the night in the jungle. He missed his wolf family, and Bagheera and Baloo.

Mowgli felt tears running down his face again. But he knew he had to get used to living outside the jungle. The man village was his home now.

Life in the man village was very hard at first. There were a lot of things Mowgli had to learn, especially talking in man language.

Often, Mowgli would get his words wrong. The other children laughed at him. This made Mowgli very angry. In the jungle, no one laughed at anyone if they got something wrong the first time.

Sometimes, he got so angry, he was tempted to hit the other children. He was much stronger than they were. But Bagheera had taught him to control his temper. He would never show those children that they were hurting him.

On dark nights, Brother Wolf would slink into the village. He gave Mowgli news of his family.

"What about Shere Khan?" Mowgli would ask. "Has he been seen?"

"You hurt his pride," said Brother Wolf. "He is still in hiding. But some say he swore to come and get you."

Some evenings, one of the herdsmen in the village would tell stories. His name was Buldeo, and he loved telling scary ghost stories. One night, he told one about a ghost tiger that haunted the jungle.

"What nonsense this man talks," said Mowgli to himself. "He has no idea what kind of creatures live in the jungle. He's probably never been there. There is no such thing as a ghost tiger."

The village headman could tell that Mowgli often felt sad. "The boy is not used to playing children's games. He grew up in the jungle where he had to fend for himself," he said to the other men. "He is used to the open air and to hard work. Let him be a herdsman in the fields. He will be happier there than playing games with the children in the village.

The herdsmen took Mowgli under their wing. They taught him how to look after the cattle and the buffaloes. One of

them carved Mowgli a herdsman's stick. He showed him how to use it to prod the cattle along.

Mowgli enjoyed working in the open air. He preferred being with animals than people, and they liked him, too. They would come at once when he called, and they never strayed on their way to the river.

Mowgli liked riding on the back of Rama, the buffalo. It was like riding on Baloo or Bagheera, only slower.

Sometimes, he watched Messua working in the paddies with the other women. They sang beautiful songs as they sowed the rice. Then one afternoon, Brother Wolf brought urgent news.

Mowgli was asleep in the shade of a tree. He woke up when Brother Wolf licked his feet to let him know he'd had arrived.

"Shere Khan's whiskers have grown back again," said Brother Wolf. "He has come out of hiding, and he has sworn to kill you."

"But how will he lure me back into the jungle?" wondered Mowgli.

"He is not waiting for you to come back," replied Brother Wolf. "He is coming for you here, in the fields. It will show the wolves in the pack how brave he is."

"When is this going to happen?" asked Mowgli.

"Tomorrow," said Brother Wolf.

"Then, I must act fast," said Mowgli. "I must lay careful plans if I am to defeat Shere Khan once and for all. Will you help me, Brother Wolf?"

"I shall defend you for as long as I live," said Brother Wolf.

"And I am your leader," growled a voice in the long grass. "I, too, have come to help you."

The grass parted, and Akela ambled out. He looked very old and weak. He walked with a limp. But he had fire in his eyes, which filled the others with confidence. He was still a leader.

CHAPTER 6

The End of Shere Khan

Akela suggested a very clever plan. "You must split the herd in two, Mowgli," he said. "I'll lead one half, Brother Wolf the other."

When Shere Khan came out of the jungle, he spotted Mowgli alone, riding on Rama at the bottom of a ravine. Bare rocks rose up on either side of him like walls.

"I have come to get you, man cub," growled Shere Khan, his eyes blazing with anger. "Prepare to die."

He bounded at Mowgli and Rama. Mowgli simply raised one hand and shouted, "Now!"

The ground started to shake. Pebbles rattled down both sides of the ravine. A great cloud of dust rose in the sky.

Khan stopped dead in his tracks, seeing a herd of buffalo thundering down one side of the ravine. It was led by Brother Wolf.

Another herd was coming down the other side. It was led by Akela. Before he knew it, Shere Khan was surrounded by angry, mooing buffaloes. He was trampled under a hundred stamping hooves.

When the air cleared of dust, Shere Khan lay dead on the ground. He would scare man and beast no more.

The people in the village came out to see what the great noise was. They saw Mowgli skinning the tiger. There was no sign of Akela and Brother Wolf. They had slunk back into the trees; they didn't want to frighten the children. Mowgli had calmed the herd down. The buffaloes were all munching grass, swishing their tails calmly.

"Such a beautiful tiger skin," said Buldeo. "Sell it to me. I'll give you one rupee."

"No," replied Mowgli. "I killed the tiger. It's my tiger skin."

Buldeo frowned. He didn't like Mowgli. A boy like that, who could kill a tiger, might become the headman in the village one day. Buldeo was jealous.

"How could a small boy kill such a big tiger?" he said to the other people. "He must have used magic."

"He sleeps under the stars at night," cried one of the children. "He is a sorcerer."

"He will bring bad luck to the village," shouted an old woman.

Messua pushed her way through the crowd. "You should all be grateful to the boy. He has killed the mighty tiger." She turned to Mowgli and hugged him. "Go back to the jungle," she said gently. "You will be happier there."

"Yes," cried the villagers. "Go back to the jungle where you belong. We don't want strange people here."

Some of the children started throwing stones at Mowgli. One of them hit Rama, and the beast snorted angrily.

"See," said Buldeo. "He has put a magic spell on the cattle and the buffalo. They might run away if we are not careful."

"Go quickly before they hurt you, my child," said Messua. "Goodbye, and may you have a happy life."

Mowgli gave Messua one last hug. Then, he ran across the fields. Brother Wolf and Akela were waiting for him at the edge of the jungle. Together, they ran through the trees.

Mowgli sighed happily. It was good to be back home.

Mother Wolf came out of the cave to welcome him. "I knew you would return," she beamed happily.

Father Wolf stared at the tiger skin. "And you have kept your promise," he said. "Shere Khan will trouble us no more."

That night, there was a full moon. The wolves met at Council Rock. They'd heard that Shere Khan had gone in search of Mowgli. They were expecting him back to tell them he'd killed the man cub.

Akela climbed to the top of the rock. He was quiet, but the other wolves noticed that he had a powerful look in his eyes. In the moonlight, his fur looked sleek and shiny. He was more like the strong leader they once knew.

"Listen, everyone," called Akela. "I have great and important news."

The wolves all fell silent. A shadow floated out from among the trees. The wolves gasped in surprise. It was Mowgli, walking tall and proud. He was wearing a thick cloak over his shoulders. Shere Khan had not killed him after all. Mowgli climbed to the top of Council Rock to stand next to Akela.

"The tiger came to find me," he shouted. "But I have come back to the jungle. And I have kept my promise."

Then, he unfurled his cloak for all to see. The stripes shone in the moonlight.

"See, I have killed the mighty Khan."

The wolves all stared at the tiger skin in disbelief. Then, they looked up at Mowgli as he stood on Council Rock.

"The man cub has killed the tiger," one of them said. "He should be our new leader."

"Yes!" the other wolves agreed. "The man cub is a brave and terrible creature."

"Silence," yelled Mowgli. He looked at the wolves gathered at his feet. "You are wolves. Your leader should be a wolf like you. I do not belong with you."

"Besides, you only want me in the pack now that you think I am a hero. Most of you didn't want me when I was a helpless little man cub. Akela is your real leader. He might be old, but he is wise. Do not let his wisdom go to waste. Let him lead you. As for me, I shall say goodbye to all of you."

The wolves all turned to Akela. "Yes," they said. "The tiger convinced us that Akela was weak. But his wisdom makes him strong. He shall remain our leader."

Mowgli bowed to Akela and climbed down from Council Rock.

His wolf family gathered around him. "Is this really goodbye?" asked Brother Wolf.

"I do not belong in the village," said Mowgli. "And I do not belong in the wolf pack either. I must find my own way, my own home in a part of the jungle where no one else lives. I must learn to survive by my own rules and my own strengths.

"Oh, let us come with you!" begged Brother Wolf.

"Yes!" said Mowgli, "We'll hunt together in a new part of the jungle."

Baloo came to say goodbye as Mowgli prepared to leave. "Do not forget me, man cub," he said.

"Nor me," said Bagheera. He and Mother Wolf and Father Wolf watched as Mowgli led the four cubs away.

Mowgli lived happily in a new part of the jungle for many years. He hunted with his four brothers and slept in a new cave. It is said that when Mowgli grew up, he left the jungle and started a man family. But that is another story. The wolves in the jungle still tell of Mowgli, the little man cub, who defeated the terrible tiger and brought peace to the jungle.